CLIFFSIDE

Gavin Alexander

ARTHUR H. STOCKWELL LTD
Torrs Park, Ilfracombe, Devon, EX34 8BA
Established 1898
www.ahstockwell.co.uk

British Library Cataloguing-in-Publication Data.
A catalogue record for this book is available
from the British Library.

This is a work of fiction. Names, characters and incidents are the
product of the author's imagination and any resemblance to actual
persons, living or dead, is purely coincidental.

ISBN 978-0-7223-5100-0
Printed in Great Britain by
Arthur H. Stockwell Ltd
Torrs Park   Ilfracombe
Devon EX34 8BA

CHAPTER 1

It is one minute past twelve o'clock on a very hot early July day. Paddington Station, in West London, is busy – very busy. The main concourse is thronged with people of all ages, descriptions and creeds. Some are arriving, some departing, while others stand in small groups, staring up at the Arrivals and Departures Board intently.

Katie Petherick, a young, attractive maternity nurse, has just completed her three-hour journey from Exeter, and is making her way excitedly to the departure gate of Platform 13, where she has agreed to meet William Gladly Walters, a very successful thirty-six-year-old banker, who has already made himself a fortune in the City of London. He is married to Claire, who has just produced for him a little baby girl, to be named Philippa, at the Portland Hospital, renowned for its excellence, and exclusively reserved for the progeny of the rich, rare and famous.

William, who is normally a cool customer under pressure, is concerned and agitated, on this occasion, as he has just collected Claire, Philippa and his mother-in-law, Diana, from the Portland Hospital, driven for twenty-five minutes to Paddington in eighty-nine degrees of heat, and now parked in a ten-minutes-only parking bay beside the main entrance to the station. Time is of the essence, but fortunately luck is on his side. Katie is only minutes late, and, having armed himself with the photograph that

3

she sent him previously, William soon recognises her and makes the introductions. Three minutes later, William is putting Katie's suitcase in the boot of his sparkling new Mercedes and the five of them are on their way to William and Claire's lovely three-storey house in Chelsea's fashionable Cheyne Walk. Everything has gone to plan, and a new chapter in Katie's life has just begun.

CHAPTER 2

Born in Cornwall thirty-two years ago, Katie has lived in this glorious county all her life and is very proud of her roots. Her father, Arthur, and mother, Joan, have always been tenant farmers on the Tidleyvarden Estate, in North Cornwall, owned since the sixteenth century by a family of the same name. Their 160-acre hill farm is down to permanent grass pasture, ideal for their prized herd of Jersey cows and their flock of pedigree Dorset sheep, both of which are their pride and joy.

Katie attended the village school in Tansworthy, where she was very happy, and then went on to secondary school in Bude, where she thrived. She was blessed to be born an all-rounder – intelligent, pretty, sporty and permanently surrounded by friends. She achieved six GCSEs, plus a B and 2 Cs at A level, and excelled at tennis, gymnastics, netball and judo.

Katie adored her home life on the farm, helping milk the cows, rearing and feeding the sheep, and riding her Exmoor pony, Dippy. Pony Club, gymkhanas and eventing were her passion, and she made numerous friends in the process, in all walks of life.

Throughout her life, her best and closest friend has been Sarah Tutton. They met, at the same age, at the village school in Tansworthy. Both went to secondary school in Bude, playing in the same teams, and were inseparable in everything they did.

Once their schooldays were behind them, Katie and Sarah both had to make important decisions about jobs, career paths, and making their way in adult life. For Sarah this was very easy. All she had ever wanted to do was live and work in her beloved Cornwall. She therefore opted for a secretarial course in Exeter, and a year later became PA to the senior partner at Maggots & May, solicitors in Bude, where she has worked ever since.

For Katie, however, this was not so straightforward. From an early age, probably because of her upbringing on the family farm, she dreamt of becoming a vet. But she also possessed a strong maternal instinct, a love of small children and a desire to travel. After much soul-searching, she finally decided to undertake a year's course in midwifery and maternity in Bristol.

Once qualified, and because she was ambitious, professional and dedicated, Katie made a flying start to her career, and was soon in much demand in the locality. Through her many contacts, Katie's reputation soon spread more widely, and for the last three years she has been employed throughout the UK and beyond as an upmarket monthly maternity nurse.

Ever since they finished their respective training courses, Katie and Sarah have shared a tiny isolated cottage, right on the edge of the stunning cliffs between Bude and Boscastle. Cold and windswept in winter, but heaven in spring and summer, Cliffside Cottage only has four rooms – one very small bedroom in which you can barely fit two single beds, a tiny bathroom, a kitchen and a snug – but they are blissfully happy. Completing the threesome is Ling, Katie's extremely handsome golden retriever, her constant and trusted companion, whom Sarah looks after whenever Katie is away.

Needless to say, social life for Katie and Sarah is hectic. They are both fun and attractive, and constantly sought after by the young male fraternity. Sarah has had a number of steady boyfriends over the years, but Katie has always been more reticent and aloof, for her part. However, for the last year she has had an ongoing but somewhat tenuous relationship with Peter Dunkett, who was at secondary school with Katie and Sarah, and whose father owns a butcher's shop in Bude. Peter has worked in the shop since school and is head over heels in love with Katie – feelings which are not totally reciprocated, despite the fact that they get on well together. Peter is good-looking, polite and genuinely nice, but a little dull and insipid in Katie's opinion, and aimless, lazy and without drive in his approach to life. He is the very opposite to Katie, who is always going places and getting things done.

Their relationship is now at a crossroads. Compatibility is obviously an issue, exacerbated by Peter's loathing and disapproval of Katie's continual travelling around the country, mixing with upper-crust families and staying at smart addresses. However, the biggest bugbear of all is lack of money in Peter's case. He earns a pittance in his father's shop, finds it difficult to pay the rent in his minuscule flat in Bude, and fears that he will never have sufficient funds to escort Katie down the aisle.

But Katie has dreamt up a daring and devious plan, which could change everything. It is brilliant in theory, but full of risk, and she knows that Peter will strongly disagree and disapprove of it. If it works, Peter and Katie could share the reward, and have some substantial cash in their pockets; if not, their relationship must end abruptly, and perish. This is decision time.

CHAPTER 3

Claire is thrilled to be home with little Philippa. The Portland Hospital was superb in every way, and the nurses efficient, caring and helpful, but there is nothing like one's own bed – the more so, since she was advised to have, and duly had, a caesarean operation, and is now tired and sore, needing rest, peace and quiet to fully recuperate.

Claire and William's grand bedroom is on the first floor of their spectacular Georgian town house in Cheyne Walk. The linen sheets on their giant king-sized bed are particularly inviting, the soft wool woven Wilton carpet is a far cry from the cold shiny floors of the hospital, and the full-length, bright and pelmeted curtains are a joy to see again. The walls of their bedroom are covered with watercolours of seaside scenes of Bembridge, in the Isle of Wight, where she has always been on summer holidays, and oil paintings depicting rivers, churches and rolling countryside in Norfolk, home to her as a child.

Outside the bedroom is a wrought-iron balcony, very popular in that part of Chelsea, which looks out over a large and immaculate garden, laden with herbaceous borders, shrubs, fruit trees, and a large circular fish pond with an ancient fountain in its midst.

Beyond the garden, and only a 9 iron away, Father Thames flows majestically towards Chelsea Bridge before wending his way to Putney, Chiswick, Hammersmith and Hampton Court.

Adjoining William and Claire's bedroom is William's dressing room, with its one single bed, to which he is to be confined for the duration – a thought which fills him with dread.

On the other side of their bedroom is a spacious bathroom with all the latest designs, mod cons and accoutrements. And, beyond that, a further small bedroom has been allocated to little Philippa. Katie is very pleased with this arrangement and spends time preparing the cot, checking on the baby's changing station, and putting away the pile of nappies and baby clothes.

The top floor of the house consists of three large and very comfortable en-suite bedrooms, which are normally occupied by friends, given that William and Claire are 'open house' and love their parties and entertaining. However, Katie has been allocated a room in the granny flat on the ground floor of the house which juts out into the garden. It adjoins the sitting room, which is dominated by a massive television. There William, being an avid television fan, spends most of his time in the evenings.

Denisa, their delightful Malaysian cook/housekeeper, brings sandwiches for late lunch to William and Claire's bedroom. William opens a bottle of vintage champagne, and glasses are raised to Claire and Philippa to celebrate their safe return to Cheyne Walk.

During lunch, Katie suggests a daily feeding routine, with which Claire agrees: six feeds a day at four-hourly intervals. Katie would join William and Claire for an 8-p.m. supper, and then Claire would return to bed to rest before the 11-p.m. feed. At this stage, Katie would be free to have some time to herself for a couple of hours.

The rest of day one goes smoothly, and the schedule works well. That evening, during her break, Katie returns to her granny flat, lies on her bed and rings Peter in Bude. It is a short and unsatisfactory conversation.

"Hi, Peter. How is everything in Cornwall? All is going smoothly here in London and I am getting on well with William, Claire and Philippa. I am confident that our plan will work."

"So be it," replies Peter. "But I am not, emphasise NOT, happy."

CHAPTER 4

For William and Claire, the next ten days are to be the happiest time in their married life, overjoyed as they are by the arrival of little Philippa.

Congratulatory cards and emails flood in, accompanied by regular visits from the local florist. Claire's many girlfriends come in their droves to see her, and Philippa, in the mornings, and there are daily drinks parties for William's male pals in the evenings.

Katie, on the other hand, is on edge. She is in a state of constant unease and quandary, despite the fact that she gets on very well with William, Claire and Philippa. She is now having qualms and second thoughts about the plan of action that she discussed with Peter before departing for London. It is daring and dangerous in the extreme, but the financial benefits to both of them could be massive, if successful.

To achieve her goal, Katie has previously done copious research about William on Google, concluding afterwards that he would be a prime target. In his bachelor days he was very much the Lad about Town, appearing regularly in the gossip columns and *Tatler*, and had numerous girlfriends before meeting Claire. And he continued to enjoy the high life while making his fortune in the city.

Fortunately, time passes by quickly. Katie's work takes her

mind off the target, and she is included in a lot of the daily celebrations when not tending to Claire and Philippa. There is a steady stream of William's friends coming and going, which does not exactly please Claire. Most were either at Harrow or at university in Durham with William. Amongst these are former schoolmate Sir Rupert Aynsley Bunting Bart, who has a large estate in North Yorkshire. He is noisy, fun and friendly, and flirts outrageously with Katie at every opportunity.

Another of William's friends to visit is Count Jean Michel de Rindelay, who was a student with him at Durham. He is now chairman of a large shipbroking company in Paris, married, and living in a magnificent two-storey apartment in Les Invalides. He is charming, smooth, and definitely naughty in that delightfully mischievous French way. And, no doubt, he has a string of mistresses, Katie thinks.

William has numerous cousins, one of whom is Rory O'Claverty, who also visits Cheyne Walk at this juncture. Based in County Limerick, and very Irish in his demeanour, he has oodles of charm, considers himself very attractive to women and is very entertaining. He has a 200-acre estate near Adare, where he farms, trains racehorses and runs a small stud farm.

All three of these reprobates express interest in Katie's maternity nursing services while in Cheyne Walk, which is very pleasing to her, given that they are amongst William's closest friends, that birds of a feather always flock together and that she has already unearthed plenty of useful information about William's early days in London. This gives her the hope and reassurance she needs.

It is now time for Katie to make a move on William.

CHAPTER 5

Banking and making money are William's passion in life, while watching television in the evening, after work, comes a close second. Sport of every description is his number-one viewing choice. Modern-day blue humour is also high on his list. *Mrs Brown's Boys*, which some may find distasteful, is another favourite. Katie is also a big fan of this programme, so they watch it together, laughing out loud, after supper, while Claire is resting.

In passing, William has also expressed an interest in the notorious *Love Island* programme, about which he has heard plenty, but he has not actually seen it. After supper on her last night, when Claire has retired to bed, Katie suggests that they watch a repeat. Wine, for William, has flowed freely at supper. He is keen, and soon transfixed and boggle-eyed at the outrageous antics and depraved behaviour of the young people featured. Katie sees her chance.

Now dressed provocatively in bright-blue skin-tight trousers and a low-slung see-through pink top, she gets up from the sofa, slips deftly round the back of William's chair, puts her strongly scented hands through his blonde hair, opens the top two buttons of his shirt and whispers in his ear, "We too could behave badly together, William, and nobody will ever know."

Now fortified by yet more wine, William is caught unawares

and puts up minimum resistance. Katie takes him by the hand and steers him towards her bedroom in the granny flat. Undressing speedily, she is soon stretched out full length on the bed – her lithe, bronzed well-formed body and ample bosom in full view. William is smitten, stripped naked in a flash, and slips in beside her. They are quickly wrapped around each other – arousal, erection, climax and consummation being achieved in minutes. Pure lust on William's part – emotionless ulterior motive on hers. She lies still, victorious, £ signs winging through her mind. William switches from ecstasy to panic in a trice, now guilt-ridden and horrified by what he has done. He re-dresses quickly, climbs the stairs and shuts himself in his dressing room, now shaken to the core.

The next morning a taxi arrives in Cheyne Walk to take Katie to Paddington, en route to the West Country. William, Claire, Philippa and Denisa stand on the doorstep to wave her a fond and very grateful goodbye.

By mid-afternoon Katie is back home in Cornwall.

CHAPTER 6

Katie is thrilled to be home. There is nothing more inspirational than summer in Cornwall. It is exceedingly hot, the azure sea glistening in the sun, a cool breeze wafting back over the mainland. Sarah is not yet back from work, but Ling is overjoyed to see Katie, almost knocking her over as he bursts with abandon from his kennel. She texts Peter, suggesting that they share a takeaway supper in his flat, to which he agrees.

Katie is planning to have six weeks' holiday at Cliffside Cottage, having worked without a break since Christmas. She takes Ling for a long walk along the cliff edge and down the steep winding path to the beach below. Ling is beside himself with excitement, dashing crazily along the sand and headlong into the sea beyond.

Sarah is back when they return to Cliffside Cottage, and over the moon to see Katie again. They hug each other tightly, chatter and laugh incessantly, catching up on their respective lives in the two weeks since they were last together.

Later that evening, Katie is anxious, and she has mixed emotions while driving to Bude to see Peter. She is looking forward to seeing him, but uneasy and on edge about how he will react to her fleeting association with William. She prays that he will understand, forgive, and see the big picture. She talks; he listens in silence, his eyes staring straight in front of him, his hands clasped and shaking. He is visibly shocked, ashen white, and trembling with indignation, but, thank God, ultimately convinced and reassured when Katie explains that £10,000 will be paid by William into her bank account, for his misdemeanours. The atmosphere is tense, but Peter's mood improves a little after a bottle of white wine, a spoiling Thai curry and a warm embrace.

Bridges have been mended. Peter reports that he will be windsurfing with pals for the next three evenings, and they plan to spend time together at the weekend.

Katie drives back to Cliffside Cottage, greatly relieved that her evening with Peter has ended well. She tiptoes into the bedroom, where Sarah is fast asleep, undresses, squeezes Sarah's hand briefly, and falls asleep herself.

CHAPTER 7

The next morning, Katie and Sarah have breakfast together before Sarah leaves for work in Bude. They chat about possible activities in the evenings for the rest of the week – tennis, walking on the cliffs and beach with Ling, and a girlie supper party at Cliffside Cottage being their preferred options.

Katie's focus and objective for the day is writing a letter to William in London. It will need a great deal of thought, and must give him no means of escape. Amid much cursing, and after screwing up three draft copies, she finally comes up with a format and wording which will suit her purpose.

Dear William,

I loved my two weeks in London with you, Claire and Philippa, and cannot thank you enough for your kindness and hospitality. You are a charming family and I am particularly fond of Claire, with whom I got on very well. But it is for this reason that I have had two sleepless nights back here in Cornwall, tossing and turning, and thinking about our brief but illicit encounter on my last night. I have a deep-seated conscience about what happened between us, and feel very strongly that Claire should know the whole story. However, the choice is yours. If you can live with your guilt, so be it. But, if so, I must insist that you make me a sizeable payment if I am to remain silent. My fee for two weeks' maternity nursing is £5,000, but I would suggest that you transfer £15,000 to my bank account to honour our agreement. My sort code and account number are below.

With best regards to you all,

Katie.

Katie then takes Ling for a long walk along the cliffs, posting the letter in the little hamlet half a mile from the cottage.

On her return, the telephone rings unexpectedly and a voice at the other end she does not immediately recognise says, "Hello, Katie. It is Rupert Aynsley Bunting here. You and I met briefly when you were doing your maternity-nursing stint with William and Claire in London. Forgive me for ringing out of the blue, but I was wondering if you could do me an enormous favour. As I told you at the time, my wife, Camilla, is having a baby in two weeks. She is to be induced. We booked a monthly maternity nurse from Yorkshire months ago, but, sadly, the poor girl has gone down with chickenpox and will not be able to come to us. It's very short notice, for which I must apologise profusely, but is there any chance that you could help us out?"

Katie thinks quickly, very tempted by the request, and jumps at the opportunity.

"Hello, Sir Rupert. Yes, I do remember you. In fact, I was planning to take two months' holiday in Cornwall, but, in the circumstances, am happy to come, given that you are a close friend of William and Claire's."

"That would be marvellous," replies Sir Rupert, now mightily relieved. "I will check the train times from King's Cross to York and tell Hargreaves, my butler, to fetch you from the station in one of my Range Rovers on the day that I collect Camilla from the hospital in Harrogate. Could you please make enquiries about train times from Exeter to Paddington that would coincide? Camilla will be thrilled, and it will be fun. I will ring you again next week with more details, and to firm up arrangements."

Katie puts down the telephone and spends the next thirty minutes googling Sir Rupert on her computer. She concludes that this will be another prime opportunity, and not one to be missed.

It has been a very satisfactory day: one large fish caught, netted with no way to escape, and now another, in Yorkshire, firmly on the line.

CHAPTER 8

Having made the impromptu decision to go to Yorkshire, Katie is determined to make the most of her next ten days at Cliffside Cottage. The weather is glorious and there is always so much to see and experience in Cornwall at this time of year.

Sarah takes a few days' holiday from her job in Bude, and they plan an action-packed programme, incorporating all the things they like doing together. Tennis, walking on the cliffs and beach, and a couple of girlie supper parties are already inked in, and now waterskiing on the Camel river at Rock, a Cornish cream tea in Boscastle and an evening out at their favourite restaurant at Padstow are added to the list. Cliffside Cottage will be 'open house' for the next ten days, and Ling will be beside himself to have Katie and Sarah at home together.

Katie's weekend with Peter in Bude goes fairly smoothly, and they have a fun time together. Peter is more relaxed and accepting of the status quo, in the knowledge that he is going to receive half of the proceeds that Katie has demanded from William. It is still hard for Peter to come to terms with his plight, but he believes this is the only way that he will accumulate enough capital to marry Katie, whom he adores.

On their first evening, Katie shows Peter a copy of the letter she has written to William demanding the money. And, after supper, she tells Peter about her imminent and unexpected assignment in Yorkshire with Rupert Aynsley Bunting. She explains that she has googled Sir Rupert, and, given his lifestyle and implied reputation, this must be another opportunity for further deceit and skulduggery. Peter goes quiet for a moment, taken aback by this latest development, but he regains his composure when reassured by the financial benefits in store. It is obviously unfortunate that Katie will have to miss out on two weeks at Cliffside Cottage, but there will always be other occasions when they can be together.

Towards the end of her ten-day break, Katie receives a telephone call out of the blue from a man with a smart French accent.

"Is that Katie? This is Jean Michel de Rindelay here. We met in London, when you were working for William and Clare in Cheyne Walk, and you very kindly gave me your contact details. This is very much a last-minute request, but would there be any chance that you could come to Paris for two weeks at the end of August? My wife, Françoise, is having a baby. We already have two children, aged five and three, and have come to the conclusion that our nanny, Sylvie, might not be able to manage a newborn baby as well. She is a lovely person and has been with us for six years, but is sixty-five years of age and not as active as she was."

Katie is caught unawares, but knows that she has to make an instant decision. Her gut feeling is that she should accept, for obvious reasons.

"Hello, Count Jean Michel, I was actually planning to be on holiday at that time, but would be happy to change my schedule in view of your close friendship with William and Claire. Furthermore, I have never been to Paris and this is a heaven-sent opportunity."

Count Jean Michel is thrilled, and much relieved, promising to email Katie in a couple of days with travel options and more detailed information about her stay in Paris.

Katie puts down the telephone, a little dazed by this latest train of events, but elated by the thought of two weeks in Paris. She has had a blissful ten days with Sarah, and everything seems to be fitting into place in her professional capacity as well.

And it is about to get better. That evening an online bank update reveals that William has transferred the £15,000 into her account as demanded. Her first big fish has been safely landed.

CHAPTER 9

Katie is on her way to Yorkshire. Cornwall apart, it is her favourite county in England. She has been there several times before, and has been captivated by its people, its landscape and its charm. She is sitting in a first-class compartment, which Sir Rupert has insisted upon, aboard the mid-morning express train from Bristol to Paddington. From there she will take the short underground ride to King's Cross, and catch an InterCity train to York. Her destination is Badlersdale Park, which stands majestically in the stunning countryside of North Yorkshire, between the towns of Malton and Pickering.

The long journey between Bristol and York goes smoothly, and John Hargreaves, Sir Rupert's butler, is there to meet her outside the station in the second of Sir Rupert's Range Rovers. Born and bred in Yorkshire, John is very proud of his roots, of Badlersdale Park, and of the fact that he has been butler there for thirty-five years, now with Sir Rupert and previously with his father, Sir Edwin. He is dressed very smartly in a tailor-made tweed suit, checked shirt, British Field Sports Society tie, and immaculately polished brown brogue shoes. Jolly, affable and articulate, he and Katie chat without a break, all the way. He is obsessed by Badlersdale Park – a magnificent country mansion set amidst an extensive rural estate of farms, wood and parklands, only a few miles from the North Yorkshire Moors. It is one of the finest examples of the work of the celebrated architect James Paine, built in that splendid Palladian style, so much admired in the mid-eighteenth century.

He tells Katie that he is one of three permanent staff at Badlersdale Park – the other two being Grace, the cook/housekeeper, and Olive, the housemaid – all of whom live with their families in the servants' wing of the house.

Meanwhile, Sir Rupert is on his way back from the hospital in Harrogate with his wife, Lady Camilla, and little James, who was born two days earlier weighing an impressive eight pounds and nine ounces. The two Range Rovers arrive almost simultaneously, and Camilla's mother, Adonia, is there at the front door to greet them, gesticulating wildly with Jeremy, aged six, and Amanda, aged four, James's two older siblings.

It is now 6 p.m. Katie goes with Camilla and James up to the master bedroom on the first floor of the house, and Sir Rupert suggests that everyone should congregate in the drawing room at 7 p.m., to be followed by dinner in the dining room afterwards.

Camilla helps Katie to unpack and arranges everything neatly in James's little bedroom and the bathroom between. Sir Rupert will base himself in his dressing room while Katie is in residence. Katie proposes a baby-feeding schedule, which Camilla agrees to very quickly, having already produced two older children. All is going to plan, and everyone is happy.

It has been a long day, but Katie has a very positive vibe about the next two weeks. Badlersdale Park is a wonderful place. Her nefarious tactic is now tried and tested, and there is every possibility that there is more bounty in store.

CHAPTER 10

Time passes apace at Badlersdale Park, and young James Aynsley Bunting has the most perfect start to his life. Camilla and Katie gel well together, while Camilla's mother, Adonia, is thrilled to be supervising and caring for her two older grandchildren, Jeremy and Amanda.

Camilla is a likeable but very unusual person. Small and a little rotund, with short-cropped brown hair, she is studious, artistic and very content doing things on her own. She enjoys reading, particularly historical novels, plays the piano beautifully and is very knowledgeable about gardening. The view from Rupert and Camilla's bedroom is one to die for: a long pristinely mowed lawn, edged by two rectangular colour-graded herbaceous borders sloping gently down towards a large, spectacular and well-stocked lake with park and woodland, and the North Yorkshire Moors beyond. It is quite simply idyllic.

Sir Rupert is a different kettle of fish: only thirty-six years old, but still living in the nineteenth century in essence. He is a large man, distinctly portly, and has bright-red flushed cheeks, the result of good living, drinking copious amounts of whisky and red wine – and partaking of the occasional snort of something naughty, no doubt. He is very set in his ways, which are not to be changed greatly on this occasion by the arrival of his third child. Breakfast, lunch and dinner are all eaten in the dining room –

the last-named a formal affair, with John Hargreaves attired immaculately in black jacket and striped trousers, and Olive, in a black dress with white apron, in attendance throughout.

Katie's bedroom is also on the first floor of the house, but in a different wing, the corridor leading to it being dimly lit and rather spooky. As a result, she spends as little time as possible there, when not with Camilla and James, preferring to socialise with John, Grace and Olive in the kitchen. Olive is particularly chatty, and enjoys regaling Katie with anecdotes about the many parties that Sir Rupert has hosted at Badlersdale Park over the years. Most have been riotous affairs, with a great deal of drink taken, incorporating very rowdy and sometimes outrageous behaviour, almost always with Sir Rupert at the helm. Needless to say, this is music to Katie's ears.

Every morning after breakfast, and ten minutes spent with Camilla and James, Sir Rupert drives his Range Rover around his estate, checking on the health of his herd of prize pedigree Jersey cows, admiring his four hunters, now back at work after their summer holidays, and being updated by his farm manager on the state of the harvest, which is still in full swing. Following lunch, he browses the *Daily Telegraph* briefly, and falls asleep in his favourite chair in the library prior to spending the rest of the afternoon driving around his extensive partridge and pheasant shoot, in discussion with his gamekeepers, and shooting pigeons, which are the bane of his life.

And – of particular interest to Katie – after dinner every evening, when Camilla goes for her rest, he always takes his Range Rover for a final spin around his estate, to see that everything is in order before he retires to bed.

Could this be Katie's opportunity? She thinks long and hard. Time is running out. The fish is circling, but not taking the fly. Her only chance is to engage Sir Rupert in conversation during dinner, and so far this has not happened. With only days to go, however, her luck changes. At long last, Sir Rupert invites her to sit beside him at the dinner table. This is crunch time – sink or swim. It is a fun evening and very relaxed. John Hargreaves keeps Sir Rupert's glass well filled with red wine, and after the main course Katie seizes her chance and takes the plunge.

"Sir Rupert, I have loved being with you, Camilla and James at Badlersdale Park – it has been a privilege. But there is one big favour I would like to ask. I was brought up on a farm in Cornwall – my mother and father are still tenants on the Tidleyvarden Estate. They have a herd of pedigree Jersey cows, which are their pride and joy, and I would love to see your herd before I leave. I have noticed that you always go for a quick spin around the estate after dinner, when Camilla goes for her rest and before you retire to bed yourself. Would it be possible for me to come with you? My mother and father would be thrilled, I know."

Sir Rupert is taken by surprise, but reflects quickly, his eyes lighting up as he speaks: "Katie, that would be fine. Let's do this after dinner on your last night. It would give me a lot of pleasure," he adds tellingly. "I have always wished that Camilla would show more interest in my prize cattle."

CHAPTER 11

Dawn is breaking on Katie's last day at Badlersdale Park. She has not slept well. She is on tenterhooks, and has been kept awake by the enormity of what lies in store. Pent-up anticipation and excitement on one hand; the fear of failure, embarrassment and degradation on the other. With hindsight she can see that her brief encounter with William in Cheyne Walk was reasonably straightforward; tonight's assignment with Sir Rupert will create a far greater challenge.

Spending time with Camilla and little James steadies her nerves through the day, but dinner cannot come soon enough. Two male cousins of Sir Rupert's have been invited and are placed on either side of Katie. Both are extremely dull, and difficult to communicate with, which does not help the situation. Sir Rupert sits between Camilla and her mother, which makes Katie feel uneasy, guilt and conscience building up inside her at the thought of her impending dalliance with Sir Rupert later in the evening.

Grace cooks a delicious culinary triple-header of twice-cooked cheese soufflé, grouse and banana fritters – but these are wasted on Katie. She cannot wait for dinner to finish and for everyone to leave the table. At last Camilla goes up to bed, the guests depart, and Sir Rupert makes ready for his regular evening excursion. He slings his blazer and tie on a wooden chair in the hall, and motions to Katie to get into the front passenger seat of his Range Rover.

"Jump aboard, Katie. Let's get going. Apologies for my two cousins – they are both very nice people, but unbelievably boring. Takes all sorts – I prefer those with a bit of spark about them. We have three ports of call – my Jersey cattle, my hunters and, lastly, a brief glance at the pheasant poults in Jubilee Wood," says Sir Rupert.

"Sounds good to me," replies Katie.

This is action stations. Sir Rupert follows the long drive past the lake, and heads for the parkland beyond. He is delighted that someone is showing such a keen interest in his prize Jersey cattle. They jump out of the car and gaze admiringly at the herd, munching contently on their lush green pasture. Sir Rupert is in his element, advising Katie about the welfare, feeding and pedigrees of his cattle, while Katie reminisces about the happy days she spent, in her youth, on her father's farm.

'A positive start,' thinks Katie to herself, gaining in confidence and ready to up her game as they drive on to view the hunters, half a mile away.

"That was brilliant. My mother and father will be so pleased that I have seen your Jersey herd," says Katie, putting her hand on his left arm in a nonchalantly tactile thank you.

He does not flinch. She drops her hand deftly to his knee and squeezes gently. No objection there either.

"I am passionate about my hunting and am adamant my hunters have a long relaxed break at the end of the season," says Sir Rupert as they stand looking over the fence in admiration.

"I rode from the age of three and love horses," replies Katie, the two now talking nineteen to the dozen as they return to the car on their way to Jubilee Wood. "Thank you, Sir Rupert. That was special," says Katie, her hand returning swiftly to his left knee and this time venturing up his inside leg.

Sir Rupert does not resist.

"I would now like to show you my young pheasant poults, which were delivered this week and are now running free in the release pen in Jubilee Wood. We will leave the car beside the shooting hut in the middle of the wood, where we have lunch on shoot days," says Sir Rupert.

They park and approach the pen. It is getting quite dark by now.

"Sadly, we won't be able to see too much, which is a shame. I love this time of year, when the pheasant poults arrive."

They chatter non-stop, but the light is fading fast.

"Would there be time to have a quick look inside the shooting hut?" asks Katie as they make their way to the car.

"Of course, Katie!" exclaims Sir Rupert. "But there is a little logistical problem, which I think I can solve. There is no electricity or lighting in the shooting hut."

He bends down, removes a key from underneath a large urn beside the front door of the shooting hut, unlocks it and walks gingerly to the far end, stopping in front of a large open fireplace with a long wooden mantelpiece above it, two enormous white pillar candles standing at either extremity. He fumbles in his pocket, finds his cigarette lighter and ignites both candles.

He turns to face Katie, now only feet away, standing seductively, her scanty blouse and bra removed, to reveal her firm ample bosom. Sir Rupert is transfixed, hands trembling at his side in anticipation, his eyes jumping gleefully from their sockets. She undoes her short skirt, which falls swiftly to the floor, and Sir Rupert is overcome by the beautifully honed body which lies beneath. He is mesmerised – putty in her hands. She undoes his shirt and unzips his trousers. Within seconds, they are both standing naked together, his rampant weapon now massively erect, protruding proudly beneath the folds of his large stomach. Katie swings her legs over the side of the long pine table, and in no time at all is lying prostrate, enticing her prey. He throws himself upon her, writhing and roaring, as if in deference to the stags whose heads hang dolefully round the walls of the shooting hut. Ejaculation and consummation are immediate. The deed has been done.

Nothing is said between them as Sir Rupert and Katie make their way back to Badlersdale Park. The light over the front door shines brightly. Everything is quiet. Sir Rupert climbs the stairs wearily to his dressing room, now stunned by what has happened, lost in guilt and confusion.

Katie finds her way to her bedroom, negotiating the long spooky and dimly lit corridor in her wing of the house. She is elated, her mission accomplished. Another large fish has been caught and netted.

CHAPTER 12

It is as if nothing has happened. Sir Rupert sits at the head of the dining-room table, supping his coffee and perusing his *Daily Telegraph*. Scrambled eggs, bacon, black pudding, tomatoes, mushrooms and fried bread perch invitingly in their steaming silver salvers on the sideboard while John and Olive busy themselves, scurrying between kitchen and dining room as always. The only change to the daily routine is that it has been decreed by Sir Rupert that breakfast should be at 8.30 a.m., not 9 a.m., so that John and Olive can clear away in time for John to drive Katie to York Station.

As John carries Katie's suitcase to the Range Rover, Sir Rupert, Camilla, James in her arms, Jeremy, Amanda and Adonia gather together at the front door to say their goodbyes and thank yous.

The journey to York goes according to plan, Katie and John locked in conversation throughout. When they first met, John had given Katie a brief overview of Badlersdale Park, but this time he is more specific, regaling her about the detailed history of the house, Sir Rupert's countless ancestors and the magnificent paintings which adorn its walls. Having left in good time, John and Katie arrive punctually at York Station fifteen minutes before departure. John gives Katie a farewell peck on the cheek – they have become firm friends over the last two weeks.

Sitting comfortably in her almost empty first-class carriage,

Katie reflects on her stay at Badlersdale Park as the InterCity train hurtles through Doncaster, Grantham and Peterborough on its way to King's Cross. It has been a memorable experience in so many ways. From a maternity-nursing perspective it has been a pleasure to be with Camilla and James, while her bank account could be about to benefit from another sizeable jackpot. The game plan is working – it is almost too good to be true.

On the second leg of her journey, from Paddington to Exeter, Katie's thoughts turn to Cornwall and her next week at Cliffside Cottage. She is longing to see Sarah, and to spend time with Ling, who is so much part of her life. The only blot on her landscape is Peter. She spoke to him twice while at Badlersdale Park, but their conversations were fraught and unsatisfactory. He had been offhand, curt and critical – as if something was troubling him. Is it because he is missing her, she wonders, or is there a hint of jealousy appearing? She is concerned, and sends him a cosy text suggesting they speak later in the evening.

Summer is still in full flow as Katie crosses the River Tamar into Cornwall. Its narrow roads and little seaside villages are crammed with cars, caravans and tourists, the latter overwhelmed by its allure and charm. Sarah has not yet returned from work when Katie reaches Cliffside Cottage, but Ling is there to greet her, tail wagging furiously, and jumping with joy. She takes him for a walk along the cliffs, and Sarah is there when they get back. They indulge in a long and affectionate hug, open a bottle of rosé, and swop their news over a crab supper.

Before going to bed, Katie takes her mobile into the garden and rings Peter. It does not go well. He is monosyllabic, unenthusiastic and not interested in hearing about Katie's stay in Yorkshire. They agree to see each other later in the week, but there is now a definite cooling in their relationship.

CHAPTER 13

Katie has a lazy next morning, getting up late and taking stock of the situation, helped by three large cups of coffee, and Ling, who lies contentedly beside her.

Peter is a worry, but she is determined to try and repair the damage. She is still fond of him, but they seem to be drifting apart. Their meeting later in the week will be decisive.

Her two weeks in Yorkshire have been very productive, and she must now consider how best to demand her payment from Sir Rupert for his unwise misdemeanours. She thinks it through, concluding that the letter is best left for a few days, to comply with her narrative.

She is now looking forward to Paris – a city she has never been to before. She googles Count Jean Michel, and is happy with what she reads. He is very wealthy, lives life in the fast lane, and could be another one ready for the picking. Peter will not be pleased that she is going to be away for another two weeks, on yet another mission, but so be it.

Summer is almost over, so she wants to spend as much time as possible at Cliffside Cottage with Sarah and Ling. They have agreed a load of things to do together, including a two-night stay with Katie's mother and father at the farm at Tansworthy. She has not been home for a while, and this must be remedied.

The postman calls later in the morning with a letter for Katie, postmarked 'Southern Ireland'. It is from Rory O'Claverty – a formal embossed invitation to his thirty-fifth birthday party, including dinner and dancing at the Dunraven Arms in Adare, County Limerick. It is accompanied by a card from Rory written in his own hand.

Dear Katie,

Herewith is an invitation to my 35th birthday party. I very much hope you can come. When we met in Cheyne Walk, you told me that you had never been to Ireland – this will be an excellent opportunity to put this right. We will have a fun and riotous Irish party which you will love. Attractive girls will be in demand! There are lots of my friends staying in my house, and you are welcome to join them. There is a daily flight from Newquay to Shannon, which will be perfect. I will arrange for a taxi to meet you. And bring your jodhpurs and boots.

Katie is taken by surprise, but flattered to be asked, and excited about the thought of two days in Ireland, about which she has heard so much. She ponders, and decides to sit on the invitation for a few days.

Katie has a blissful week, but with one exception: her evening in Bude with Peter is disastrous. Conversation in the restaurant is stilted and you could cut the atmosphere with a knife. Peter just cannot come to terms with the situation, but insists that he is still madly in love with her. He is incensed that she is now going to Paris for two weeks, but, nevertheless, he still wants to see her when she returns. The omens are not good. The situation seems hopeless. Katie is determined to accept Rory O'Claverty's invitation, whatever Peter might think.

All is now set for two weeks in Paris. Count Jean Michel has sent Eurostar tickets and detailed arrangements for her stay. Only one more thing to do – write her letter to Sir Rupert.

I just loved my two weeks with you, Camilla and James, who is an adorable little boy. Badlersdale Park is the most wonderful place, and John, Olive and Grace were extremely helpful and friendly to me. However, I now have a problem – a serious one – with which you must help me. I have been contacted by the editor of a London tabloid newspaper, who wants to publish a story about you and me. It would appear that someone was watching when we were in the shooting hut together after dinner. He has offered me £10,000 for an exclusive revelation. I don't want to do this and would hate to tarnish your name and reputation, but it is a lot of money and I am struggling financially at the moment. My bill for maternity nursing for two weeks is £5,000. Could you please transfer £15,000 to my account to compensate me, and put an end to the matter? I very much hope so.

Best wishes,

Katie.

CHAPTER 14

"My first time in Paris! This is going to be an adventure. Yippee!" Katie is talking to herself ecstatically as the midday Eurostar pulls out of St Pancras Station, accelerating through the East End of London and Kent's Garden of England to Dover. And on then, under the Channel to Calais, and across the flat landscape of Northern France to the Gare du Nord. It is an exhilarating journey.

Count Jean Michel de Rindelay has instructed Katie to take a taxi from the Gare du Nord to his home in Les Invalides, in Paris's fashionable Seventh Arrondissement. It is a frightening experience. The driver of her 'yellow peril' is a swarthy, bespectacled, blue-beret-wearing young Frenchman, smelling stenchingly of garlic and Gitanes. He drives like Jehu, weaving in and out of traffic at great speed, oblivious of other drivers and all-unsuspecting pedestrians, hurtling down the Rue La Fayette, the Avenue de l'Opéra, and the Rue de Rivoli to the Place de la Concorde at the bottom of the Champs-Élysées. Katie is absolutely terrified, holding on grimly to her seat for all she is worth, and is mightily relieved when her maniac driver crosses the River Seine, via the Pont de la Concorde, and comes to a grinding halt halfway down the Rue St-Dominique, close by the Hôtel des Invalides.

"*Nous sommes la!*" he exclaims triumphantly – the only three words he has uttered since leaving the Gare du Nord.

Katie vows never to travel by taxi again in Paris.

Fortunately, things improve on reaching her destination – a grand two-storey apartment on one side of a magnificent rectangular courtyard, built in classic style at the beginning of the nineteenth century. Count Jean Michel's aristocratic family have lived very comfortably in Paris for many generations, and he is also the owner of a lovely chateau in Normandy in addition to villas in Provence and Guadeloupe, and a chalet in Verbier. He answers the front door himself, dressed impeccably in bright-red well-tailored trousers and blue tight-fitting jacket. He is very good-looking, athletic and oozes charm. He introduces Katie to his two elder children, Melvin and Benoit, and to Sylvie, their loyal but now elderly nanny. He brought his wife, Françoise, home from hospital earlier in the afternoon, along with their newborn daughter, Nicole. They are now comfortably settled in the master bedroom and pleased to meet Katie. Both Count Jean Michel and Françoise speak perfect English, which comes as a massive relief to Katie. Katie and Françoise make themselves acquainted and agree a routine for the upcoming two weeks with which they are both happy.

Count Jean Michel then shows Katie to her bedroom, on the same floor. It is small, but en suite, and very comfortable. Martinique, the middle-aged Algerian-born housekeeper, brings her supper on a tray while Count Jean Michel and Françoise have theirs alone in their bedroom.

It has been a long but enjoyable day – her twenty-minute taxi ride from the Gare du Nord apart. She is looking forward to the next two weeks, and to what might lie in store. The omens are promising, and she has a positive vibe.

CHAPTER 15

Badlersdale Park and Les Invalides in Paris are poles apart – not only in mileage, but in their lifestyles and daily routines. Count Jean Michel is an ambitious and very successful man. He is chairman of the Societé Rindelay, one of the largest shipbroking companies in France, their Central Paris office being in the Rue St-Honoré, adjacent to President Macron's Élysées Palace. He gets up promptly every morning at 5.45 a.m., and spends half an hour in the gym on the lower floor of his apartment. He is put through a rigorous fitness regime by Angeline, his twenty-nine-year-old fitness instructor. She is pretty, fit, well muscled and very sexy. Katie bumps into her every morning as she busies herself with Françoise and Nicole at their 6-a.m. feed – and they dislike each other intensely from the outset. Angeline is obviously enraged that another good-looking young female has invaded her territory.

After a meagre breakfast of fruit juice and filter coffee, Count Jean Michel then walks briskly to his office, over the Pont de la Concorde, which takes him precisely twenty minutes. He excels at tennis and skiing, and has five horses in training with top trainer André Fabre, in Chantilly. He is passionate about art, and has a fine collection of Impressionist paintings in his apartment, by Matisse, Cézanne and Picasso. He spends little time at home, despite being the new father of his third child, being permanently tied to his office desk through the day when not partaking of lengthy lavish business lunches and dinners. He is very much his own man, and likes himself a lot.

His wife, Françoise, is eleven years older than her husband, still very elegant, but not as attractive as she once may have been. She is well read, refined and sophisticated, but arrogant, self-centred, and demanding in equal proportions. Her relationship with Katie is cordial, but restrained. She admires her as a maternity nurse, but treats her as an inferior. It is not ideal, but Katie accepts the situation, her mind focused on the main chance: her intended misbehaviour with her husband, Count Jean Michel.

Katie does her job to the best of her ability as always, but pines for her free time, after Nicole's 2-p.m. feed, and the daily opportunity to see and investigate Paris while Françoise is resting. Les Invalides is the perfect place to explore from, the Louvre, Eiffel Tower, Champs-Élysées and Latin Quarter all being within easy walking distance. She is intrigued and overwhelmed by the charm, character, history and people of this unique city, and vows to return.

However, there is one major problem: her two-week stay in Les Invalides is almost over, and she has had no chance to communicate meaningfully with Count Jean Michel. He leaves early in the morning, is committed to his business through the day and comes home late in the evening, when Françoise expects him to spend time with her and Nicole, on their own.

Lady Luck is to play her part. That evening, Count Jean Michel returns home a little earlier than usual and comes across Katie looking at his pictures in the hall.

"Hello Count Jean Michel. I am so impressed by your magnificent paintings – I would love you to tell me about them," says Katie eagerly.

"Now is not the best time, Katie, but we could possibly do something tomorrow, which I think will be your last day with us. I have a little studio on the top floor of an old apartment block on the Quai d'Orsay, overlooking the river. I do some painting there myself, purely as an amateur, and would be delighted to show you some of my sketches and to give you a short overview of the Impressionist era. I have a lunch organised with business clients, but could possibly find time afterwards. I will give it some thought, and push a note under your door before I go to bed," replies Count Jean Michel, charm personified, his blue eyes lighting up perceptibly and his body language speaking volumes.

Katie is beside herself with excitement. A chink of light – a last-minute chance to cast her spell!

Count Jean Michel is true to his word. Later that evening, as Katie is turning her light out, an envelope appears under her bedroom door. She opens it, her hands trembling.

'Come to my studio on the Quai d'Orsay at 3 p.m. tomorrow afternoon. I will be there. I will text you the address and apartment number tomorrow morning.'

Is it going to happen? Katie turns over and closes her eyes, but cannot sleep.

CHAPTER 16

It is ten minutes to three on Katie's last day in Paris. Nicole has had her 2-p.m. feed; Françoise is resting. Count Jean Michel has texted, and she is now on her way to his studio on the Quai d'Orsay. She presses the door buzzer in the street outside. It opens immediately, and she takes the lift to the fifth floor and knocks on the door of the studio.

"Come in Katie," says Count Jean Michel, charming as always. "I am so pleased that you are showing so much interest in my paintings, and that you have come to my little studio this afternoon. I am passionate about fine art, and love to dabble in a little painting myself – views and scenes in Paris mostly, and sketches of pretty girls on occasions. He guides her round the little studio and through the glass double doors, which are open wide, on to the balcony beyond. It is the most spectacular and inspirational view of Paris, overlooking the majestic River Seine. Katie is bewitched, but struck by the shambolic state of the studio. It hasn't seen a Hoover or a mop in ages, and is littered with dilapidated easels, old paintbrushes, half-used paint pots, discarded sketches and piles of rubbish. An unmade sofabed strewn with out-of-date magazines and filthy painting rags is in one corner.

Count Jean Michel is wearing shorts and a T-shirt, his blue city suit and tie hanging tidily behind the door.

"As it is your last working day in Paris, would you like a glass of champagne? I am going to have one," he says.

"Not for me, Count Jean Michel, but I would like a cup of coffee," replies Katie.

They sit beside each other on two rickety old wooden chairs, in the middle of the studio, chatting effusively. Conversation comes easily. They bond, enjoy each other's company and move closer together. He looks longingly into her eyes and admires her perfect body.

"You are the most beautiful girl, and it is such a shame that I have hardly spoken to you while you have been in Paris. I would adore to do a quick sketch of you standing in front of the double doors to the balcony, the city of Paris behind you. I will obviously pay you for this – and more, if you are prepared to pose naked."

"That is fine by me, on both counts. How much will you give me?" replies Katie.

"Five thousand euros," suggests Count Jean Michel tentatively.

Katie returns his stare. "Ten thousand euros and I will do it, naked as you wish. And another 10,000 euros if we have sex," says Katie.

They shake hands. The deal is done.

Katie undresses. Count Jean Michel is enraptured, paintbrush in hand and at the ready. She poses seductively, hands on hips, the Paris skyline behind her.

'It is going too well,' thinks Katie. 'There must be a setback coming soon.'

How right she is! At that very moment there is a thunderous crashing on the door of the studio, which is thrust off its hinges, a flimsy bolt falling pathetically to the floor. It is Angeline. She is aghast, shaking with rage, venom coming from her every orifice.

"How dare you, Jean Michel! Katie is an English pig and nothing like as attractive and sexy as me."

He is speechless, taken totally by surprise.

"And you are a foul little French slut," interjects Katie defiantly.

Angeline removes her leotard, bra and knickers and stands naked, and full frontal to her employer.

"Look at me – you know that I am right," she shouts. She pushes him to one side and confronts Katie, eyeball to eyeball, their suntanned bodies rammed together, breasts clashing. "I want to fight you, to teach you a lesson," screams Angeline.

"That is OK with me," Katie shouts back.

"Beware, Katie! Angeline is very strong, and a qualified judo instructor," adds Count Jean Michel, sensing danger.

"I am a black belt in judo. Let's do it," retorts Katie.

The challenge is on. The stage is set. Katie is taller, longer in the leg, more agile, and has a longer reach. Angeline is smaller, but thicker-set, with immensely powerful thighs and upper body. Angeline taunts Katie, slapping her in the face – once, twice and a third time. Neither gives an inch. They step back from each other for a brief moment, prowling, circling like rutting stags, feigning, parrying, and waiting for the precise moment to pounce. They lock horns, straining every sinew of their immaculate bodies, standing their ground. No quarter will be given.

They are evenly matched. It is relentless. Flurries of intricate holds and counter-holds proliferate; throws and falls come thick, fast and furious; submission is neither contemplated nor tolerated. It is a fight to the finish.

Count Jean Michel is spellbound, riveted and mightily aroused, unable to comprehend what is unfolding before his very eyes. He is overcome by lust and passion, rampant sexual urges welling up inside him. He cannot restrain himself, nor resist any longer – chucking his shorts and T-shirt to the floor, he joins the fray with relish, his now erect and throbbing weapon fully primed, thrusting here, there and everywhere. It is a maelstrom of ecstasy, a conflagration of sexual carnage, such as he has never witnessed before. And he has seen plenty.

The conflict continues unabated, bodies tumbling, twisting and contorting for all they are worth. Blood is pouring from Katie's nose; four large bite marks are embedded in Angeline's ample right breast.

The pace is manic from the outset, and exhaustion at long last takes its toll. Count Jean Michel's weapon is finally, and unceremoniously, unloaded.

All three fall back numbed and exhausted on the sofabed. Not a word is said. Count Jean Michel walks back to his office, Angeline drives to her next fitness appointment, and Katie is back in good time to help Françoise with Nicole's six-o'clock feed.

Pour ceux qui habitent Paris, la vie est different.

CHAPTER 17

Three slices of luck greet Katie the following morning as she is completing her final maternity duties before departure. First, Count Jean Michel has to leave the apartment at 5.45 a.m., before anyone is about, to be driven to an important business meeting in Rouen. Secondly, Angeline is not therefore required to oversee their normal daily fitness session, thank God. And thirdly, Françoise has instructed her chauffeur to drive Katie to the Gare du Nord, thereby removing the need to risk her life with another lunatic Parisian taxi driver, about which she is massively relieved.

Unlike her goodbyes in Cheyne Walk and Yorkshire, the adieus in Les Invalides are more formal and very low-key. Françoise gives Katie a cursory shake of the hand, with a modicum of thanks, Katie kisses little Nicole tenderly on the cheek, and the front door of the apartment is closed squarely behind her.

Pierre, the chauffeur, is charismatic and likeable, and drives very sensibly, thank goodness. He speaks excellent English, and points out well-known Paris landmarks en route. He also suggests that, as Katie is in very good time and has not had the chance to taste local French cuisine, she should sample a light lunch in one of the little brasseries opposite the main entrance to the station. Some escargots, perhaps, followed by *rognons de veau*, with a glass of *vin blanc*, to celebrate her first visit to Paris.

Katie is much taken by his suggestion, and does just that. It is an uplifting experience and a great deal better than the ageing cheese baguette she would have bought in the Eurostar terminal.

Her Eurostar train is on time and the journey passes by quickly. She sits in the window seat, next to an elderly, well-educated and, at first sight, austere-looking French lady wearing a full-length black coat, her long silvery-grey hair swept back in a neatly tied ponytail. She lives in Neuilly, in the Sixteenth Arrondissement, a much sought-after part of Paris, and is on her way to see her daughter and son-in-law, for whom Parson's Green is now home. As it happens, Katie's initial impressions could not have been more wayward – her new-found French friend is charming, and wonderful company. She tells Katie about her childhood in Northern France, through which they are now passing, and her early memories of Paris during the Second World War.

On the opposite side of the table are a middle-aged couple who hail from Kentucky, in the USA. Both are wearing Stetson hats and talking non-stop in that delightful Midwest drawl. They have stayed at the luxurious George V Hotel, just off the Champs-Élysées, and been sightseeing, eating and drinking to their hearts' content for two days. They are now on their way to London for two nights at the Ritz Hotel in Piccadilly, to complete their European odyssey. They are hilarious and obviously enjoying every minute of their holiday, inviting Katie to stay with them in Louisville at any time she wishes.

The second leg of Katie's journey back to Cornwall is less frenetic, the Paddington-to-Exeter fast train being surprisingly empty. Her thinking is dominated by two specific subjects, both of which have to be addressed.

The first is Peter, and their future relationship. While in Paris, Katie has sent him two very amicable texts, both of which he has ignored. She now sends him another, suggesting that they meet locally at a neutral venue, to clear the air. She is determined to remain on friendly terms with him, whatever happens.

Her mind then turns back to Count Jean Michel and the tumultuous fracas in his studio the day before. It should never have happened, Angeline's disgraceful behaviour being totally out of order and beyond all belief. If only she could have had sex with Count Jean Michel on her own, as he had agreed prior to Angeline's disastrous and uncalled-for arrival, there would never have been a problem. She thinks it through at length, coming from every angle, finally concluding after considerable self-cross-examination that Count Jean Michel had definitely been part of a sexual act with her, but with another person participating. This is beyond doubt. The letter she intends to write to Count Jean Michel will make this abundantly clear, and that must be the end of the matter. He must pay up – end of story.

This constant soul-searching depresses Katie, but, nonetheless, the journey ends on a positive note. A glance at her mobile shows that there has been a credit transfer into her online bank account – a payment from Sir Rupert of £15,000. Eureka!

Two large fish have now been successfully landed and another has been caught and netted.

Katie is back at Cliffside Cottage in time for a poached-egg supper. Sarah greets her with a long embrace, and Ling is thrilled to see her. They chat without stopping, Katie giving Sarah a detailed account of her two weeks in Paris, albeit it an abridged version.

CHAPTER 18

The next morning Katie takes the lazy approach to life, intent on recharging her batteries after her eventful two weeks in Paris. It is Tuesday, and she is counting down the days until the weekend, when she will fly to Ireland for Rory O'Claverty's party. He has sent a text asking her to make a booking on the Saturday midday flight from Newquay to Shannon, where Donal McKelway, a much liked local taxi driver will meet her. She can't wait.

However, her top priority for the time being is her upcoming meeting with Peter, which she is adamant must be at a neutral venue, and somewhere they don't usually go to together. Texts are exchanged between them, and it is agreed that the old coastguard station at Braniston Point will fit the bill. It is a thirty-five-minute walk for Katie from Cliffside Cottage, and only a ten-minute drive from Bude for Peter after he finishes work at the butcher's shop at 5.30 p.m.

Nine times out of ten, when going for a walk with Ling, Katie turns left out of Cliffside Cottage, from where the cliffs begin to descend gradually past the hamlet of Trebiston to the beach below. Instead, this evening she takes a right turn towards Braniston Point, a well-known local landmark, home to puffins and gulls, where there is no beach access. Instead there is a fairly sheer drop to rocks and sea below. She follows the cliff path with Ling, apprehensive, her mind confused, and deeply troubled by what lies ahead.

Peter's car is already parked in the tiny visitor's car park, where the lane ends, only yards from the cliff's edge. She continues on the rough track past a little copse to the old coastguard station, a stone's throw away. It is an oval white-painted building with a glass dome. In use for many years, the building is now redundant, shabby and in very poor repair. Protruding from its front is a small square red-brick hut, from which coastguards used to keep watch through long, thin rectangular slits in the brickwork. It would have been the perfect vantage point to spy German warships in the two world wars, and invading Spanish galleons centuries before.

Peter is standing at the door of the hut, and he gives Katie a fleeting kiss on the cheek. The hut is dark and dank, and littered with dust-covered bottles and old crisp packets. The only furnishings are a grimy collapsible wooden table in one corner and a long cold concrete bench beside it, on which they perch. Conversation is stilted, monosyllabic. There is no empathy between them – none at all.

"How are you, Peter?" asks Katie, impatient to break the ice. "I loved Paris. It is a wonderful city. I sent you two texts while I was there – why did you not reply?"

"I am gutted, Katie. My life is hell. When you are away I miss you terribly, and just want to block you from my mind. I cannot carry on this way any more. Can we spend a weekend together at my flat and try to put things right?" says Peter.

Katie is stunned, stymied, with no way to escape. She has to explain.

"Peter, I can't. I hate to tell you this, but I have been invited to a party in Ireland on Saturday. I have accepted – I am going. I am very sorry."

Peter is speechless, his lips twitching, his face crestfallen and his brain in neutral.

"Katie, how can you do this to me? You know that I am mad about you."

Katie knows that this is the end of the road, but does not want to hurt his feelings.

"Peter, I am going, and that is that. I think it is best that we don't see each other for a while. If there is still a flame burning, it will reignite, but only with time," says Katie.

No more is said. They leave the hut and go their separate ways.

CHAPTER 19

Sarah knows Katie better than anyone. She has been a bosom friend since their early days at school, so, as soon as Katie stumbles through the front door of Cliffside Cottage, on returning from her meeting with Peter, she is certain that something is seriously wrong. Not only is Katie soaked to the skin by rain, but she is also pale, shaking and unwilling to speak.

"Where have you been, and what have you been doing, Katie? You are not your normal bubbly self. Please tell me – I just want to help," says Sarah.

"I have been to the old coastguard station at Braniston Point, to meet Peter. And it could not have gone worse. He is in the depths of depression, bitterly aggrieved that I am spending so much time with smart people, away from Cornwall. He just cannot steer his head around the fact that my job as a maternity nurse entails regular two-weekly sessions with families all over the country, and beyond. He wants me to spend the weekend with him in his flat in Bude, but I cannot as I am going to a party in Ireland on Saturday. That has upset him even more as he is now very jealous of me and my lifestyle. Our relationship is at a crossroads, and it is getting me down, big time," says Katie, pulling herself together with difficulty.

"Men – they can be a pain in the arse," says Sarah. "They want everything to go their way, and get stroppy and bitter when it does not. He will have to accept the situation if he wants the relationship to continue. He is a likeable fellow, and you have been friends for a long time, but there are plenty more fish in the sea."

They have a hot shower, open a bottle of white wine, cook spaghetti bolognese for supper, and watch a movie on television, curled up on the sofa in the snug.

"To hell with the male sex!" they conclude. "As long as we can be together and have fun at Cliffside Cottage, we will be happy."

Katie's mood improves considerably the nearer she gets to start time on Saturday. She buys herself a new lace cocktail dress in Padstow, tickled that it is appropriately green and fits to a tee. Then she writes a carefully crafted letter to Count Jean Michel confirming the deal that they made in his Paris studio, before the fracas, from which he cannot escape.

'London, Yorkshire, Paris and now Ireland – most people would give their bottom dollar to sample this quartet of mega centres in the space of six weeks. You have to take the rough with the smooth. Roll on the Emerald Isle! Here I come,' Katie muses to herself contentedly.

CHAPTER 20

The county of Limerick is covered by a thick blanket of Irish mist as the daily flight from Newquay nears Shannon Airport. Katie is staring intently through the little porthole window, but the patchwork of tiny fields and spread fences is barely visible below. She will have to wait until the plane lands before discovering the lush green landscape and undoubted charm of the Emerald Isle.

The plane is only half full, and the terminal almost empty, so immigration and customs procedures are completed in no time at all. As Katie leaves the arrivals hall Donal McKelway is there to greet her with his blackboard held aloft, Katie's surname scribbled on it in white chalk. From the outset, it is apparent that Donal is a tremendous character. He is small, vastly overweight, with bright-ginger hair, and he is dressed in a pair of poor-fitting grey shorts, and a sickly green T-shirt boldly emblazoned with 'You just cannot beat County Limerick'

"Hello, Katie. I hope you have had a good flight. Welcome to County Limerick, and may God be with you while you are in it," says Donal with a broad smile.

"It is brilliant to be here. I have heard so much about your lovely country," says Katie as she steps into Donal's little yellow taxi.

The journey from Shannon Airport to Rory O'Claverty's home,

Ballybillbastion Court, between Adare and Rathkeale, takes thirty-five minutes and is non-stop entertainment. Katie begins the conversation by asking about his family and upbringing, Donal seldom drawing breath from then on.

"I was born in a little village between Limerick and Adare, the youngest of nine children. I went to school in Limerick, never learnt a thing, but loved all sports and was high-jump champion in my year."

Katie interjects, "But, with the greatest of respect, Donal, you are very small. How could you be so good at high jump?"

"I was a great lepper – that is the secret to my success," replies Donal. "Limerick is a wonderful city on the banks of the River Shannon. You must experience it while you are here. Irish coffee, which is made with Irish whiskey, was invented there, and the city is famous for its sizzling food, its street art, and its rugby legends. And you must visit King John's Castle – a local landmark since 1210. It is brilliant."

At this point, Donal stops his taxi by the side of the road in the middle of nowhere.

"You see that old horse, leaning his head over the fence over there? He won the Grand National when he was younger. You must go and congratulate him," says Donal.

Katie gets out of the taxi and does what she is told.

"I gather from Donal that you won the Grand National," she says.

"Ah, for God's sake, you must not believe him. He has always been a terrible liar," replies the horse wearily.

Katie jumps back into the taxi, cursing Donal, but tickled by his quirky Irish sense of humour.

Donal carries on, without drawing breath: "I hear from Rory that he is having a big birthday party this evening at the Dunraven Arms in Adare. I will be driving yous all there and back in my minibus. You will have a great time. Adare is one of Ireland's prettiest villages, founded in the thirteenth century. The

Dunraven Arms is a grand hotel. The food is tip-top, and it is the perfect place for a party. And Rory loves a bit of craic."

At that moment, Donal takes a right turn off the main road through some old wrought-iron gates into Ballybillbastion Court, a small late-eighteenth-century mansion overlooking the Shannon Estuary. It is a fine-looking building, but has seen better days and is in need of some urgent TLC. The front of the house and the driveway are cluttered with cars belonging to guests staying for the party. Rory is at the front door to greet Katie.

"Welcome to Ballybillbastion Court. Great that you could come! We are all having a cup of tea, but will be moving on to the hard stuff very shortly." He introduces Katie to his wife, Mathilde, and to his other guests, all of whom are itching for the celebrations to begin.

After tea, Rory takes Katie through the large kitchen into the cobbled stable yard, horses' heads peering over their stable doors. Hunters would have been housed here in the old days; finely tuned thoroughbreds now occupy every one of the thirty boxes therein. They continue to one end of the yard and up a steep flight of stone steps to a well-appointed guest bedroom on the first floor, which would have been the huntsman's living quarters originally.

"Make yourself comfortable, Katie. Have a bath if you want and a little rest so that you are ready for the fray later on. We will meet back in the drawing room at 7 p.m. for a glass or three of champagne before leaving for the Dunraven Arms. I hope you have brought your jodhpurs and riding boots, as I suggested," says Rory.

"I will, and I have. Can't wait," replies Katie.

She falls back on the bed and closes her eyes, excitement welling up inside her at the thought of the party, and riding out the following morning.

The only thing that puzzles Katie is why Rory has invited her to the party in the first place. It seems very strange.

CHAPTER 21

Katie is back in the drawing room at the appointed time, dressed to perfection in her new green cocktail dress, hair immaculate and looking her best. Heads turn as she enters. The menfolk are all wearing dinner jackets; the girls are decked out in their finery. The room is filled with chat and laughter, champagne flowing – and a bevy of dogs, of all hues, sizes and breeds, duck and dive around and between people's legs on the mud-spattered floor.

Rory is holding court by the mantelpiece at one end of the room. Portraits of his ancestors, in massive frames, look down at the ensuing party with pride. He is, to borrow that hackneyed cliché, tall, dark and handsome – charm personified to the fairer sex, and the envy of most men. Oozing bonhomie, he is the archetypal Irish carouser. He read land economy at Trinity College Dublin, but had an aversion to his studies, preferring to enjoy himself with his many and diverse friends. He played rugby for his university, and later for Munster, and was a proficient point-to-point rider in his late teens. Training racehorses is now his passion, and he is one of the up-and-coming masters of his craft, nurturing the budding careers of both Flat and National Hunt horses very successfully, and earning glowing tributes from the racing media.

Swiss by birth, Mathilde is standing at the other end of the drawing room, a little overcome by proceedings. She and Rory met at university, fell in love and married soon afterwards. At the time, they seemed to have much in common, but their lives have been drifting apart in recent years. They have no children. She pines for Geneva, dislikes County Limerick and its inhabitants, and has a hatred of horses. She is easy on the eye, but pin-thin and in need of a three-month diet of Guinness and Irish meat pie. Her face is drawn and pale, and her hair prematurely grey, not improving her overall appearance. Rowdy parties and dancing are not her thing. Her number-one interest is classical music, and she enjoys attending concerts in Dublin, London and Vienna. She has already arranged for Donal to collect her from the party at midnight, two hours before the designated 'Carriages at 2 a.m.'.

At 7.45 p.m. Rory claps his hands together, gives a shrill wolf whistle and announces an immediate departure. Donal is standing at the front door, minibus at the ready. There is constant chatter throughout the fifteen-minute drive to Adare, the only interruptions coming intermittently from Donal, on his intercom, eager to join the celebrations and determined to air a few Irish jokes en route.

"Have you heard the story about the Irishman, the Scotsman and the Englishman who have a good few pints of Guinness in the pub, entering into a fierce argument about which one of the three is the bravest?" asks Donal. "Well, I'll tell yous anyway. Things are getting a little heated, and the poor unfortunate barman, worried that there might be fisticuffs, thinks of a way to solve the conundrum. He tells them that there is a very smelly pig in the pigsty behind the pub, and suggests that whichever of the three can stay the longest in the pigsty with the pig should be the winner. They agree. The Scotsman goes in first, but lasts only two minutes. The Irishman, determined to better this, holds his nose determinedly and staggers out after five minutes. It is now the Englishman's turn. He enters the pigsty cautiously, and the pig comes out. And, by the way, Katie, he came from Cornwall!"

Donal is delighted with himself, needless to say, most of Rory's house guests being English.

They know how to host a party at the Dunraven Arms, and everything is in pukka order, and prepared to perfection on their arrival. They are given the warmest of Irish welcomes, including buckets of champagne on ice, and happy, smiling and professional staff on hand. Dinner is announced and served – a veritable feast of quails' eggs, smoked salmon and cod's-roe salad, boeuf Wellington; and lemon, almond and blackberry roulade, to be helped down by some superb Sancerre and claret, in magnums.

Katie has the perfect draw – Brendon, on her left, who owns a restaurant in Limerick, and Dermott, whose IT company is based in Mallow, on her right. They are both hilarious, regaling Katie with numerous stories and anecdotes throughout the evening. Brendon, who was best man at Rory and Mathilde's wedding, toasts the birthday boy, everyone in stitches. Other drink-infused guests grab the microphone afterwards to add their respective two pennies' worth. The disco springs into action, coloured lights flashing (rock music mostly, just the occasional smooch). The dance floor is heaving from the outset, Katie never off it. The craic is great.

Towards the end of the evening, Rory seizes his moment for just one dance with Katie: 'Lady in Red' by Chris de Burgh, his favourite song and singer. He holds her tight, looking into her eyes, passion welling up inside him.

"I am so thrilled that you could come. It has made my evening. You don't know how much this means to me," he says, entranced.

Katie is lost for words, danger signals flashing.

The rock music resumes. Noise levels rise. Sweating bodies whirl, heave and twist. The last hurrah as 2 a.m. approaches – it has been one hell of a party! Local guests depart amid much hugging and kissing, and Donal drives Rory's now weary house guests back to Ballybillbastion Court for one more bedtime tipple.

"Sleep well, everyone. Let's have brunch at 11 a.m. I will go out with the first lot of horses, and you can have a lie-in," says Rory.

Katie retires to her guest bedroom above the stable yard, undresses, her head hitting the pillow in no time. There is a knock on the door, which pushes open. It is Rory. He stands at the end of Katie's bed, removing his black tie a little sheepishly.

"I just wanted to tell you that the first lot tomorrow morning will go out at 8.30 a.m. You will be riding Never Dilly-Dally, a four-year-old gelding who is due to have his first race in ten days' time. He is a lovely young horse, well mannered and a very good ride. You will really like him. Paddy Bernakin, my head lad, will tack him up for you. I will give you a call at 8 a.m. to check you are awake," says Rory.

"Thank you, Rory. This evening has been brilliant, and I can't wait to ride out with your string tomorrow morning. But should you really be here in my bedroom? What would Mathilde think?" says Katie.

"Mathilde came home early from the party, and will be fast asleep. I have something important to tell you, but it must wait until after first lot tomorrow. Now is not the time. Sleep well," replies Rory, shutting the door behind him.

The boot is on the other foot, it now appears. The hunter has now become the hunted. It is not what Katie might have expected.

CHAPTER 22

Rory's early morning call is not needed, as Katie is already awake at seven thirty. She has been roused from a deep slumber by the sound of an old metallic feed barrow being trundled round the cobbled stable yard as Paddy, the head lad, gives the horses their breakfast. This is accompanied by a cacophony of hollering, snorting and munching from the inmates, their light steel shoes scraping impatiently at their stable doors.

Katie lies on her bed in contemplation, elated at the thought of riding out with Rory's string, but apprehensive about what he has to tell her later in the morning. She puts on her jodhpurs and boots. Now looking the part, she descends the steep stone steps and is in the yard for eight fifteen.

Rory and Paddy are standing in the middle of the yard, chatting in general about the horses and the morning's exercise programme in particular.

"Good morning, Katie. Hope you slept well. This is Paddy Barnakin, my head lad, who will look after you. He has tacked up Never Dilly-Dally for you – by the way, he rides him out most mornings, so knows him very well," says Rory.

"Hello, Katie. Great to meet you. Never Dilly-Dally will be the perfect ride for you. He is kind and has a wonderful temperament. He moves well and has excellent manners," says Paddy.

"That sounds fine to me," replies Katie. "But I am a little

concerned. I have ridden ponies since I was a child, and then eventers, but I have never been on a racehorse."

"That will be no problem at all, Katie. He will look after you. When we canter, just take a firm hold of the reins and give him his head. You will be fine. I will be riding the lead horse, Stand to Attention, so will be there to help if needed," says Paddy.

"There are four of you to go out for exercise this morning, Katie. Paddy and you, plus Eamon and Padraigh. They are both riding young horses, which need a little time. You will have a walk and a trot in the paddock, go down the lane by the river, and then have one steady canter to the top of the all-weather track. It is seven furlongs, with a gradual climb. Paddy will lead, and you'll sit second, with Eamon and Padraigh bringing up the rear. I will follow in the Land Rover on the tarmac road, alongside you," says Rory.

Rory gives everyone a leg up and away they go. Katie is in good company. Paddy, who was brought up with horses in County Limerick, spent fifteen years with legendary trainer Dermot Weld on the Curragh before joining Rory as head lad, when he started training seven years ago.

Eamon has a solid background with horses, and was with the equally brilliant trainer Jessica Harrington for ten years prior to his arrival at Ballybillbastion.

Padraigh is only twenty-four. He did a twelve-month course at the renowned Irish Racing School in Kildare. He is a very promising young jockey.

The banter between the three lads is incessant – mostly about their Saturday evenings in the pub, and which horses they will be backing in the betting shop that afternoon. Katie is feeling a lot more confident by the time they approach the bottom of the all-weather track.

"What should I be doing now, Paddy?" enquires Katie.

"Just cock your dock, sit still and enjoy yourself," replies Paddy.

Everything goes to plan. Katie is exhilarated by the experience, and Rory is there to greet them when they pull up and take a turn round the collection ring.

"How was that, Katie? Everybody else OK, lads?" asks Rory.

"I loved every minute," replies Katie.

"Take his saddle and bridle when you get back to the yard, Katie, and Paddy will deal with the rest. I will see you there," says Rory.

CHAPTER 23

Rory drives into the stable yard, arm out of window, just as Katie is coming out of Never Dilly-Dally's stable.

"You did really well, Katie. Jump in. Let's go and have a quick look at my stud farm. It is only five minutes down the road. We will be back for brunch with the others at eleven," says Rory.

"Sounds good to me," replies Katie.

"You ride very nicely, and should do this more often. You could ride in an amateur's race one day," says Rory.

"You are pulling my leg, Rory. No way am I good enough," says Katie.

They are at the stud farm in no time, parking beside the stud buildings in front of a neatly fenced paddock in which some well-bred mares, heads down, are grazing contently.

"I have four mares, three yearlings and four foals on the place. Siobhan looks after them, and also mucks out some of the racehorses in the stable yard in the morning. This works perfectly," says Rory.

"How lucky you are, Rory, to be training racehorses and have a stud farm as well, in such a wonderful part of Ireland!" says Katie.

"I so wanted to show you the stud, but had something else to tell you about, which will not be easy. Sadly, Mathilde and I are not getting on. We are drifting apart, and our marriage is not going to last. She longs for her native Switzerland, and she dislikes County Limerick, most of my friends and anything to do with horses. She spends her time going to classical concerts in capitals all over Europe. We don't have a life together any more. It cannot go on like this," says Rory.

"I am so sad to hear this, Rory. I hate these situations," says Katie.

Rory continues: "Ever since I first met you in Cheyne Walk with William and Claire, I was obsessed – mad about you. Furthermore, you are fun, attractive and love horses. It breaks my heart that Mathilde does not take an interest in, or support, my training business. I must see more of you, Katie."

"This has come as a massive shock to me, Rory. It cannot work. You live in Ireland; my home is very firmly in Cornwall. What is more, I have a long-time boyfriend, who lives nearby. He is already very jealous of me and my lifestyle. He was furious when I told him that I was coming to a party in Ireland, and God knows what he might do if he finds out that I am befriending another man," says Katie.

"It is now five to eleven, Katie. We must get back to Ballybillbastion for brunch. But first I have an idea. I am booked to fly to the West Country on Wednesday morning to look at some young store horses. I could come back via Bude, and we could meet somewhere quiet, close to where you live. I could then stay the night in Padstow and fly back from Newquay to Shannon on Thursday morning," says Rory.

"I need time to think about this, Rory. I will text or email you tomorrow morning, once I am safely back at Cliffside Cottage," says Katie.

Rory puts his arm tenderly around Katie's shoulder and they return to the car. They walk through the front door of Ballybillbastion as Rory's house guests are coming down the stairs, in dribs and drabs, bleary-eyed – and nicely hung-over, needless to say.

"Everybody sleep well? Some of us have been up with the lark, and been out first lot with the horses. I think we all need a hair of the dog," says Rory, popping open a bottle of chilled champagne. "A scrummy cooked brunch will put us all right, and we can then continue last night's festivities," says Rory.

Katie is now exhausted both mentally and physically, and relieved when Donal arrives to drive her back to Shannon Airport. Rory escapes momentarily from his friends to bid her a brief but very fond farewell.

Donal hardly ever draws breath, as always. Katie listens, her mind far away. The plane is only minutes late taking off, and she is back at Cliffside Cottage in time to take Ling for a walk along the cliffs.

It has been a crazy twenty-four hours, and she has so much to ponder and think about. She cooks herself a hasty boiled egg, leaves a message for Sarah, who is out for supper, collapses on her bed and falls asleep.

CHAPTER 24

Social life for Katie is complicated, and becoming more so by the day. It's not what she might have envisaged a couple of months before. Two strong cups of coffee are needed to stimulate her brain and kick start her concentration.

Her relationship with Peter is on hold, with little expectation of renewal. And now Rory has launched himself on the scene like a bolt from the blue. It is very flattering, but fraught with danger and difficulties in every respect. Does she really need to have a fling with another man when she is so happy with Sarah and Ling at Cliffside Cottage?

On the plus side, her maternity-nursing business is thriving, bookings continuing to flood in on a regular basis. And, on checking her online bank account, she sees that Count Jean Michel has made the bank transfer that she demanded, for his misdemeanours in Paris. This element of her life could not be going better.

She sends Peter a friendly text, safe in the knowledge that he will not reply: 'Hope all is well with you. So strange not to be seeing you, but know that we are right to be having a month apart. Time can be the healer, and we must remain friends, come what may. Love, Katie.'

And then an email to Rory, which is more difficult.

First, many thanks for inviting me to your birthday party at the Dunraven Arms. A wonderful evening, and hugely enjoyed. As was my ride on Never Dilly-Dally yesterday morning. I have been thinking very hard about tomorrow, when you come to the West Country to see store horses. It is far from straightforward, but let's meet at 5 p.m., if this works for you. At Braniston Point, on top of the cliffs, only four miles south of Bude. You will find it easily on your satnav. There is a little car park at the end of the lane, by the cliff's edge. I will be waiting for you by the small copse of bushes, fifty yards from the car park, on the path leading to the old coastguard station nearby. It is off the beaten track, and we should have it to ourselves. It is imperative that we are not seen together. News travels very fast in this part of Cornwall. I will walk there with Ling, my golden retriever, from Cliffside Cottage. Text me if there are any problems.

Regards,

Katie.

Katie spends the day deep in thought, giving Ling a long walk and doing a bit of shopping in Bude, which includes buying prawns from the fishmonger and some fresh lettuce and tomatoes from the market stalls. She is looking forward to catching up with Sarah and taking her mind off men.

"Hi, Sarah. Brilliant to see you – a rarity these days. I had a lovely time in Ireland, but am always pleased to be home. Life is less complicated, and no hassle. The Irish are a crazy bunch of people – very likeable, and thrive on parties – but you can't beat the peace and quiet of Cliffside Cottage," says Katie.

"How's Peter?" asks Sarah, sensing that Katie is uneasy. "I have not seen much of him recently. Is everything all right between the two of you?"

"We are going through a rough patch at the moment, but hopefully we can iron out our differences in time," says Katie.

"I have noticed that you have not been your normal bubbly self of late. I thought something must be bothering you. I hope it all works out. Let's have some supper here again tomorrow to cheer you up. I will buy some sea bass in Bude. I am planning to leave work early and play some tennis. I will be back by six o'clock," says Sarah.

"Good plan. I have a busy schedule tomorrow afternoon, but will aim to be home by six o'clock too," says Katie.

They share a bottle of white wine, and chat till late, reminiscing about happy bygone days. Katie regains some of her sparkle, but is still deeply concerned about what lies in store with Rory the next day.

Life on Katie's riverbank is changing fast. Three large salmon have been safely landed, but her latest fish has turned the tables and is playing an entirely different game. He has jumped out of the river, grabbed her rod, and is casting his own fly with intent and precision, and no lack of determination either.

What will tomorrow bring?

CHAPTER 25

It is 4.30 p.m. on Wednesday. Katie is setting off with Ling up the cliff path towards Braniston Point, just as Sarah is returning from her two-hour-shortened day at the office, to change for tennis.

She waves to Sarah, shouting a cheery, "See you at six."

Sarah gives a demonstrative thumbs up in response.

It is a dull September day – no rain, and visibility is good. Katie and Ling go at a brisk pace and are there bang on time for her assignment with Rory. There are no cars in the car park overlooking Braniston Point. She and Ling take the little path towards the old coastguard station, and sit down on the solitary bench on the edge of the small copse. Rory texts – he is on his way, but twenty minutes late. This is unfortunate, thinks Katie, already on edge at the thought of their meeting.

Rory finds his way to the little cliffside car park, thanks to his satnav, parks his car, sees Ling running around and heads for the copse.

"So sorry I am late, Katie. The traffic was very busy between Okehampton and Bude." He holds Katie's hands tight, and gives her a kiss on the cheek. "I have had a productive day, looking at store horses around Exmoor and Dartmoor, but couldn't wait to see you. How was your day?" says Rory.

"It's been quiet, but relaxing. I just love being at Cliffside Cottage and having Ling for company," says Katie.

Katie likes Rory, and enjoys his sense of humour. Conversation comes easily. Laughing and joking a lot, Rory tells Katie about his childhood in County Limerick, his university days at Trinity College Dublin, and the exciting times he is having, training racehorses at Ballybillbastion. Katie relates stories and memories of her youth on the farm, life in the vicinity of Bude, and the families with whom she has been associated in her professional capacity.

Time flies by – 6 p.m. comes and goes. Rory is in full flow, and captivated by Katie. The Irish can talk, as we all know, and they can be very charming, as well.

Meanwhile, Sarah is back at Cliffside Cottage after her tennis, sharp at 6 p.m. Six fifteen passes, and six thirty, but there is still no sign of Katie. Sarah is worried, the more so given that Katie has been below par, anxious and uneasy since coming back from Ireland. She rings Peter.

"I am very concerned. Katie went for a walk with Ling to Braniston Point, and promised that she would be back by six o'clock. It is now six thirty. And she has not been her normal happy self of late."

"That is a worry, Sarah. I will drive immediately to Braniston Point and be there in ten minutes," replies Peter.

"Thanks, Peter – much appreciated. I will walk to Braniston Point and meet you. I should be there in thirty minutes."

Peter grabs his coat, and is on his way at once, driving fast and recklessly, his brain in turmoil, his anger mounting. Coming to a grinding halt in the little cliffside car park, he jumps out, noting in seconds that the only other parked vehicle has a hire-car sticker. On closer inspection, he sees that it is from Newquay Airport. A small overnight suitcase is slumped on the back seat, with a Shannon Airport baggage tag and a check-in label in the name of 'Rory O'Claverty, County Limerick'.

Peter is now convinced Katie has another man. He is incensed now, shaking with rage, putting two and two together and fearing the worst. He tiptoes stealthily to the back of the copse, peers through the bushes and spies Rory and Katie, their arms now wrapped round each other, on the bench. He creeps towards them, step by step. They are unaware. He is now only yards away, their backs toward him.

"Katie, what the hell are you doing? You should have been back at Cliffside Cottage by six o'clock. Sarah is really worried about you," he shouts. "And who are you?" He confronts Rory, who has sprung to his feet from the bench. They are eyeball to eyeball, their heads only inches apart.

"None of your business," says Rory defiantly.

"It most certainly is," replies Peter, grabbing Rory by the throat with one hand and punching him in the face with the other. Rory retaliates, and a ferocious fight ensues. Fists and feet fly, no holds barred. It is relentless. Katie is screaming, but helpless. Ling, by her side, is on guard, barking ferociously.

Both men are taking punishment, battle-worn and tiring, Rory getting the upper hand. Peter takes two paces backwards, opens his coat and pulls a knife from his pocket. He holds it menacingly above his head, hatred in his eyes. Rory retreats momentarily, now defenceless, falling backwards over the bench. Peter seizes his chance, lunges forward and stabs Rory through the heart. It is a fatal blow. Peter is adept with butchers' knives.

Peter stands, staring at what he has done, his knife embedded in Rory's chest, blood streaming from the wound. He is initially dazed, numbed, guilt-ridden, but in seconds his thoughts turn to self-preservation, and flight from the crime scene. He turns and heads towards the car park, half running, half stumbling, clutching his winded stomach, blood gushing from his bruised and battered face. Katie follows in pursuit, Ling snapping fiercely at Peter's heels.

"You are a vile, horrible man, Peter. Look at what you have done. I will make sure you pay for this. Justice will prevail," shouts Katie.

Peter reaches the car park, and his car, first. Feverishly he tries to open the driver's side door, Katie resisting with every ounce of her strength, and succeeding. He is trapped. He turns and confronts her, hatred and revenge in his eyes.

"It was all your fault, Katie. You too are going to die," shouts Peter, grabbing her viciously by the throat.

Her judo skills thwart him at first, but his superior strength ultimately prevails. They grapple desperately. This is a fight to the finish. The cliff's edge is only yards, and now feet, away. Peter is intent on throwing Katie into the abyss, Katie holding on to him for all she is worth.

But to no avail. Now they are only inches away. A moment later they topple over the cliff, locked together, falling to their almost certain death on the craggy rocks below. Lovers once, but now the bitterest of enemies.

Ling is the only witness to what has happened.

CHAPTER 26

Sarah reaches the little car park at Braniston Point five minutes later, oblivious to what has happened. It is eerily still and quiet. There is no human presence, just two cars parked randomly, one of which she recognises as belonging to Peter, and Ling, who is sitting only feet from the cliff's edge, looking out to sea, whimpering pathetically and letting out the occasional bark. He sees Sarah, bounds towards her, tail wagging, jumping up, trying to tell her something which, sadly, dog language cannot convey. Sarah senses immediately that there is something seriously amiss, fearing the worst. Ling leads her back to the cliff's edge and resumes his vigil.

Sarah is terrified of heights, but knows that she must conquer her demons on this occasion and look down over the cliff. She has to be brave. She crawls on all fours to within inches of the edge, lies full length on the ground, peers over and takes in the scene below. Now she is convinced that she can hear a frail female voice calling for help, indistinct and intermittent. Her eyes focus on a ledge fifty feet below, home normally to puffins and gulls, and strewn with little pockets of vegetation. On closer inspection, she can distinguish a human form, curled up and supported by the branches of a small tree, dressed in bright-red trousers and a short blue anorak – precisely what Katie was wearing when she left Cliffside

Cottage hours before. It must be her.

There is hope, but not for the second human form she sees lying sprawled and motionless on the rocks at the bottom of the cliff.

She inches herself backwards, still on her tummy, until she feels safe to stand. She takes her mobile telephone from her coat pocket and dials 999, her heart pounding, hands shaking. No signal. She rushes to the far end of the car park and tries again. Still no signal. Now she is overcome by fear, panic and sheer frustration. What can she do? She is alone with no form of communication to the outside world. Thinking that more height might help, she runs up the path towards the old coastguard station. And there before her, by the side of the copse, is the body of a man, slumped over the bench, a knife protruding from his chest.

"Please, God, help me, help me!" she shouts in desperation, terrified by what she has seen.

He answers her prayer, mercifully. She has a signal, and within seconds her call is put through to the emergency services' call centre. A calm and reassuring operator is asking for her precise location and what emergency services are required.

"I am at the top of the cliffs at Braniston Point. Police, ambulance and rescue helicopter are needed urgently, please. Someone has been murdered, and two people have fallen off the cliff, one of whom is caught on a ledge fifty feet below the cliff's edge. Please come quickly. I am alone and petrified. My name is Sarah Tutton. I live at Cliffside Cottage, half a mile from Braniston Point," says Sarah.

"Thank you. The emergency services will be with you shortly. Please remain calm and stay on the line until they arrive. We will continue to talk to you until then. We are professionals and used to all emergency situations," says the operator.

To Sarah it seems an age, but within ten minutes she hears

sirens and sees blue lights flashing, heralding the arrival of two police cars and an ambulance. They survey the scene, take a short statement from Sarah and are immediately about their business: cordoning off the area, examining Rory's body and taking stock of the situation at the cliff's edge.

A helicopter lands very soon afterwards in the field next to the car park, its crew highly qualified in all aspects of rescue work, which they deal with on a daily basis on the cliffs, beaches and coves of Devon and Cornwall. It is soon decided that any attempt to rescue Katie from the ledge using the helicopter would be impractical, and that abseiling down the cliff face to the ledge is the best course of action. Two experienced medics, both ex-servicemen, are in action straight away, securing a base at the top of the cliff, and bouncing down with skill and precision to the ledge on which Katie is trapped. A mobile stretcher is lowered very carefully to the two medics on the ledge. In no time, Katie is strapped securely to the stretcher and winched back to the safety of the clifftop, a medic at her head and feet. She has multiple cuts and bruises, and is very shaken, but safe, one broken leg, one dislocated arm and several cracked ribs being the initial assessment. She is swiftly transferred to the body of the helicopter, and gives a grateful little thumbs up as it takes off on its way to Truro Hospital.

It is getting dark. Arc lights are erected at the murder scene. The emergency services' vehicles depart. Two police constables are deployed to stay and keep watch overnight.

The coastguard is informed about the body on the rocks at the bottom of the cliffs. And a kind young police lady drives Sarah and Ling back to Cliffside Cottage, and stays for supper to check that she is all right.

Sarah rings Katie's mother and father, giving them a brief summary of the situation, stressing that she is safe and has now been transferred by helicopter to Truro Hospital.

Later in the evening, Sarah rings the A & E department to be told that Katie is sedated, stable and comfortable in the recovery ward, and very lucky to be alive.

Sarah is exhausted. It has been a harrowing and traumatic experience. She lies on her bed, hugging Ling, who is curled up beside her. He has been Katie's saviour – the hero of the hour. Without him, Katie could not possibly have survived.

It has been a miracle. What has transpired will only become apparent once Katie is well enough to speak to police investigators, in the morning.

CHAPTER 27

Sarah has a sleepless night, gets up early, and rings her boss at Maggots & May before he leaves home for the office.

"Hello, Mr Hewitson. I must apologise for ringing at this time of the morning. I know it's short notice, but could I please have this morning off. Katie, with whom I share the cottage, was involved in a freak and horrible incident on Braniston Point last night. She is seriously injured, and now in Truro Hospital. I have to go and see her," says Sarah.

"That is no problem, Sarah. You must go. Take the whole day off. I was expecting your call, as it has been headline news on local radio and TV," replies Mr Hewitson.

"Thank you for being so kind and understanding," says Sarah.

She then takes Ling for a two-minute spin, gives him an extra-large breakfast and a long hug, puts him in his kennel and sets off for Truro. She drives slowly, still traumatised by her ordeal of the previous evening.

On arrival at the hospital, she parks and reports to reception. She is directed to the waiting room by a jolly and efficient receptionist. A friendly A & E nurse enters only minutes afterwards.

"Would you be Sarah Tutton? Katie Petherick has told us that you might be coming to see her. She is making good progress, but I would strongly suggest that you only stay for five minutes.

She is still in a state of shock, and must rest, without any further worries or stress," says the nurse.

"Of course. I fully understand. I just want to see her – I have been so worried about her," says Sarah. "We have been the closest of friends since primary school, and have shared a cottage together for a number of years," says Sarah.

A large police constable is standing outside the recovery ward. He checks Sarah's ID and points her towards Katie's bed, which is just inside the ward. White full-length curtains are drawn right around it.

Sarah bends over the bed, gives Katie a long loving kiss and holds her hands tight.

"I have been longing to see you. I am so relieved that you are all right. You have had a ghastly experience, but it is over now. You are safe, and in the best of hands here in this hospital. I wanted to bring Ling with me, but knew that hospital regulations would not permit this. He sent his love to you this morning with a huge wag of his tail," says Sarah.

"Thank you, Sarah. I know that I am very lucky to be alive. I have had enough of men, and just want to live with you and Ling at Cliffside Cottage. I love you so much, and always have," says Katie.

"I love you very much too. We have been the closest of friends for so long, and will be very happy together, just the two of us, with Ling as our guardian," says Sarah.

Tears of joy stream down their faces. The nightmare is over. Another chapter in the lives of Katie and Sarah, at Cliffside Cottage, is just beginning.